We Fo

Maps
Keys
Hats

written by Pam Holden
illustrated by Kelvin Hawley

On Monday we went out.
We forgot to take our lunch.

We got hungry.

On Tuesday we went out.
We forgot to take our drinks.

We got thirsty.

On Wednesday we went out.
We forgot to take our jackets.

We got cold.

On Thursday we went out.
We forgot to take our
umbrellas.

We got wet.

On Friday we went out.
We forgot to take our hats.

We got hot.

On Saturday we went out.
We forgot to take our maps.

We got lost.

On Sunday we went out.
We forgot to take our keys.

We got locked out.

Today we went out.
We forgot to take our shoes.
Ow! Ow! Ow!